Echo Chamber

Also by Claire Hopple

Praise for *Echo Chamber*

"In *Echo Chamber*, Claire Hopple's precise, shimmering sentences are on full display as she explores the inner workings of these unforgettable characters. Once I started reading this book, I couldn't put it down--it's a refreshing, innovative collection."

Chelsea Hodson,
author of *Tonight I'm Someone Else*

"*Echo Chamber* is a little stinker. A fever dream, it leaves you disturbed, confused. Maybe even changed."

Tyler Dempsey,
author of *Time as a Sort of Enemy*

"*Echo Chamber* is sharp, wry, wicked fun. Claire Hopple has a light, humorous touch, but there's no question she means business."

Lindsay Lerman,
author of *I'm From Nowhere* and *What Are You?*

"Claire Hopple is a wildly talented storyteller and chronicler of humanity's inherent folly. *Echo Chamber*, her most profound and idiosyncratic work to date, is so full of wit and humor and longing that it reinforces the importance of fiction with the turn of each page. If you haven't read Hopple's work yet, rectify that mistake immediately by starting here. If you have, you are once again in for a real treat. *Echo Chamber* is nothing short of an absolute joy that should be read again and again."

Nick Gregorio,
author of *Launch Me to the Stars,*
I'm Finished Here*

ECHO CHAMBER
a novella and stories

_____

by Claire Hopple

Trident Press
Boulder, CO

ISBN: 978-1-951226-16-9

Cover by Dmitry Samarov

Published by Trident Press
940 Pearl St.
Boulder, CO 80302

tridentcafe.com/trident-press-titles

I am going to the ego circus.

—Sebastian Castillo

Is what we are related to what we have refused?

—Renee Gladman

CONTENTS

ECHO CHAMBER

CHAMBER NO. 1

She drives past the house a third time. She wants to be a natural. The blinds are closing. Maybe that's enough for today.

*

Gretchen rummages through the cupboard while the dog mashes a chew toy into her shin bone.

One thing about Marleena, she has her priorities straight, Gretchen thinks. She'd laminated a pizza delivery flier and placed it overtop her activity schedule on the fridge. Undisclosed ointments and human teeth beckon from the junk drawer. Plus, her front door is always slamming itself. And remnants of what appears to be a parade float line the basement floor.

She tucks a tissue paper flower into her bosom.

Gretchen has always been afraid that once she settles into pet-sitting for a friend, said pet will suddenly keel over in her care. What she isn't prepared for is the death of her friend while she's pet-sitting. The dog's coat has never looked shinier though.

Marleena was an elderly woman, so it could be worse. Her grown son calls the landline in striking mournful clarity. Gretchen usually thinks she can tell who's calling by the sound of the ring, but this time she's way off.

Some parents are desperate to get creative with the

spelling of their children's names but not with the names themselves. Marleena was no exception. He immediately tells Gretchen that he is Marleena's son, Frankk-with-two-Ks. He'll be there soon to settle the affairs, quell the tide of histrionic relatives, and relieve her of her dog-watching duties.

Groove is in the heart, sure, but grief is in the voice. And Frankk doesn't sound too broken up about the situation.

*

Returning from a walk with Snacks, Gretchen spies a uniformed man crouching in the grass.

He's here for the repair work on the house's foundation.

"Sorry, I got held up last week. Nice to finally meet you, Mrs. Stewart."

Gretchen mangles his extended hand.

"Please, call me Marleena."

"Well, Marleena, we have one more form for you to fill out. Paperwork. You know how it goes."

He passes her a clipboard.

Gretchen skims over the material. A bubbled floater in her eye keeps her spot on the page like a singalong video.

*

Frankk's pre-distressed jeans look ambitious.

Gretchen lets him in and offers him some gazpacho. She sits him down on the couch and heads for the kitchen.

"I'm onto you," she says into his soup bowl.

She ekes out a dollop from one of the mystery ointments. It makes a satisfactory plop when it mingles with bits of ground cumin and diced peppers.

She paws at the tissue paper flower melting into her chest from the heat of revenge.

He's swaddling himself in a dusty quilt on the couch when she enters the room.

"Best served cold," she grins.

Snacks nuzzles at her knees.

A subterranean clunking and clanging begins.

"What is that? Is someone down there?" he asks.

"A slight restructuring. Don't worry about it."

*

Gretchen knocks at the door across the street. She knows Marleena was close with the guy who lives here.

He answers. As she's explaining that Marleena has extended her trip, that he'll be seeing a lot of her in the next couple weeks, a tuft of pink fuzz flashes from behind his left shoulder.

This neighbor, Craig, is a session musician who side-hustles for a singing telegram service because it pays well. The pink gorilla costume is hands-down the most popular request. He's learning to yodel so he can add to his repertoire. Craig doesn't explain any of this to Gretchen. He doesn't know the costume's in view, and probably wouldn't tell her even if he did.

Gretchen sidles away, a little dizzy with pink possibilities.

*

Betsy was Marleena's best friend. Gretchen remembers hearing about her before. Gretchen sees Betsy's name penciled in on the activity calendar and gives her a call.

She tells Betsy the same story Craig received.

"Really? She likes it that much? She's not ready to come back?"

"It's plausible," Gretchen says.

They agree to the rec league game as planned.

"You sound young. You'll add some vigor to the court. Do some squats the day before, just in case," Betsy says, then hangs up.

Betsy immediately calls back.

"Bring your own shuttlecock."

Then she hangs up again.

The day of the match, Gretchen surveils the gymscape in front of her.

In one corner, by the vending machines, is what looks to be a field trip for bankers.

She finds a bunch of white-haired ladies stretching each other's hamstrings. She guesses which one's Betsy, waves.

At Betsy's approach, she cries soundlessly, mouth open.

CHAMBER NO. 2

Gretchen nearly concusses herself on the bedpost. With the aggressive apathy of a balloon, she dresses as a standup citizen.

Homemade jams and hypnotherapy tapes parade themselves around her lazy susan. She hears the somewhat performative murmurations of Atom, her tamed groundhog, under the stairs.

There's a commotion outside in the street. She latches her door and prowls around the corner, glomming onto the horde.

A man dislodges from the group and settles on the opposite sidewalk.

At 9:15, he extracts a receptacle from his pocket, removes what may or may not be a breath mint, and places it atop his tongue.

At 9:17, he fiddles with the buttons of a camera around his neck.

At 9:21, he yawns with his whole face.

Gretchen edges around the others for a better look at him. He looks familiar. She gives him a good once-over and he takes a photograph of her at the same time. While her head is still turned, gaspings and cheerings crackle in her right ear.

The highrise three blocks over has disappeared. She

missed the entire implosion, the whole reason for being out there, she can say that with certainty.

The man's leaving. She crosses the street, keeping him in view. He passes behind the first plaza, the second plaza, the diner, then the mall. He enters a warehouse. The door isn't locked when she catches up.

The warehouse is completely dark. She holds her arms out and centers each step in her metatarsals.

Gretchen places one palm in front of her face but it might as well not be there so she returns it to an outstretched position.

She follows his whistling.

Eventually, he slips through a back exit into daylight.

She has to fondle the wall for several minutes to find his escape, but his figure's still visible through the parking lot, a courtyard, and finally an apartment.

Nothing appears alarming as she scans his nautical-themed floor plan. She notes a life preserver and a dinghy amid other oceanic fakery on the bookshelf. He does seem like the kind who'd consider life preservation a formality.

The man eats a meatball hoagie on his balcony while she sorts through his personal effects in an orderly fashion.

In the third drawer on the left, she plunders his diary. Gretchen knows the only secrets actually kept are failures. Her fingerpads trace the trail of them framed in college rule. This record of humiliations taunts the overly ambitious.

She skims until she reaches the good stuff.

Not that anyone ever asks, but would you believe it, Valerie has put some kind of a curse on me. A real one.

She'd read the rest tonight over a glass of Canada Dry and a fresh Zebra Cake, like always.

Moving to the bathroom, Gretchen collects a sample of toe clipping specimens into a vial.

She chucks his toothbrush out the window. There'd be no more use for it after today.

His housemate mewls beside his shin because his housemate is a cat. The man is standing in the hallway.

"Coley, this is unacceptable."

Gretchen sees him clearly now. Her dentist crinkles in perturbment.

Without her asking, he starts explaining.

"Here's the thing. You can't be doing this. You're 38 years old. You're a compulsive liar. You have cavernous molars. And you're already being tailed by the police."

Gretchen picks up his floss and gets to work.

"Flattery won't get you very far, Coley."

Her bleeding gums are a dead giveaway.

"And I'm just using the name on your chart. Who knows what you really are."

The cat purrs, not reading the room.

"So get out of here. I'm gonna be late."

"What's your excuse?" she says.

"Come on. Not that you need to know, but I have an appointment with my dentist."

"I thought you were a dentist."

"And you don't think my molars need to be scraped every six months?"

They laugh.

Gretchen thinks, despite it all, they have become something like friends.

"I hope we can remain companionable."

If nothing else, she thinks she can colonize elsewhere with like-minded individuals. There's probably a whole community of people taking identities that don't belong to them. We'll swap lives endlessly until there's no trace of us left, she dreams.

CHAMBER NO. 3

Betsy encounters a youngish woman in her driveway clasping a leash connected to what appears to be a vested groundhog.

Betsy had just finished her daily recording so she had time to determine the intentions of these trespassers. Every day, she pulls out an old camcorder and reenacts her favorite episode of The Golden Girls. "Journey to the Center of Attention" now has a near-perfect rendition. She plays all the parts, everyone.

She was about to drop a check in the mail for a bounty hunting training kit when she noticed them.

"Remember me?" Gretchen asks.

Gretchen notes Betsy is wearing a sweatshirt that reads "Nanna #1" rather than your typical "#1 Nanna," which seems to imply she is one in a series instead of the best.

"That's right. You were a clear shot on the badminton court."

"Yes. Hey, do me a favor. Take Atom here for a few days, if you don't mind. I need to get away."

"You in trouble or something?"

"Not yet. Not quite. No," Gretchen says, but it could have been either one of them.

Betsy decides to expunge her record right there. Minifying her curiosity, she guides the overlarge rodent inside.

*

Gretchen figures she'll check into a hotel, then find a rather shapely pizza slice. Maybe she'll take in the theatre, who knows. Her skills in deceit aren't so different from those of a trained actor, when she really thinks about it.

Neon orange posters are stapled to every telephone pole along her path.

MISSING:
World Armwrestling Championship Bronze Medal
Issued by the World Armwrestling Federation, dated 1989

CASH REWARD. CONTACT STEVE.

Gretchen pictures a velvet rope, behind which stands a stark white monolith, empty of its treasure. But Steve isn't here to corroborate her imagination.

Sirens pull her into reality. She twitches.

A steely high-rise garnishes the corner ahead. Townes Enterprises is beplaqued near the doors.

"This looks like a real business," she says aloud.

She assumes she'll feign an appointment to get inside but the building is open and unattended.

There is in fact an empty reception area.

Gretchen settles into the seat, harnessing any vestiges of perkiness that lurk within. She is ensconced in purpose.

Pressing mystery buttons indiscriminately on the desk's panel that alight with her touch, she uncovers a hardback cinched with the telltale mylar of a library book with her other hand. It's called Introduction to Cognitive Interviewing. She flips a few pages in and learns that when interrogating suspects, one should have them draw their story backwards.

A figure pushes through the entrance.

"We need to prepare the file today. Did you have any reservations about that? Any final thoughts before we begin?" the man asks.

He doesn't seem to realize she's a stranger. He mistakes her for someone else. Or perhaps he knows exactly who she really is.

Gretchen looks at him.

"You're exasperated," she says.

He sighs, says, "Follow me."

She turns back, quickly forges her name on the inside of the book, and places it in her bag before catching up to him at the elevators.

They ascend. He starts texting. She tilts to get a better angle on his screen but can't make it out.

"Oh. I forgot you were here."

He pockets his phone.

She whispers, "What are you going to do about it?"

"We're all gathered here to make waves, to really shake things up with this client, and you want to play games?"

She grazes the elevator's emergency button, casts her eyes toward the stained carpet.

"I know," she mutters.

The doors release at the eleventh floor. He steps out and hooks a left.

Gretchen stares at a table covered in brochures as the elevator closes. She has not moved.

On the highest level, there's a round, open room offering a complete view of the city.

Gretchen's in a defunct restaurant with a gently rotating floor where occupants once gathered for brunch. She doesn't have those details, though a sudden mistrust of the floor does descend upon her. She loses all sense of orientation after a few minutes of eyeing the grid below her feet.

That's enough, she decides.

She returns to her town. Before going all the way home, she takes a trolley tour of her own neighborhood. It's loosely Country-Western-themed. She learns things she should already know that no one had bothered to tell her.

All of this information at once is too much and she starts to feel nauseous.

"Don't faint on us now," a trolley attendant tells her.

She hands Gretchen some water in a glass that's shaped like a cowboy boot.

They pass a residential street. Gretchen swears she spots a maze of shrubs in one of the backyards. Maybe the homeowner is a corn maze aficionado but enjoys participating in recreational misdirection regardless of season, she thinks.

The tour ends at the town's remarkably small zoo. A caged lioness looks inconvenienced.

Gretchen knows she'll never speak of this experience again.

CHAMBER NO. 4

––––––––––––––

The sun grazing the mountaintops wasn't visible from her window, but the spectacle playing out on her neighbors' lawn certainly was.

A man had piled up her neighbors' birdhouses and was now blowtorching them into oblivion. He is exclaiming and maybe crying.

Gretchen is accidentally impressed. She walks over to marvel at the scene.

She scans the street first. Her identity-stealing reprieve seems to have cooled tensions. Cops have quit patrolling her block at night.

As she approaches the flames, Gretchen confirms the man is wailing. She deciphers the name "Tiffany" as it repeatedly escapes his mouth.

"There aren't any Tiffanys at this residence," Gretchen tells him.

The man takes over a minute to respond.

"This is Tiffany's house. I've done my research. She was my babysitter around 30 years ago. She told me this bedtime story but my parents came home before she could finish it. She said 'To be continued' as she left, but she never came back."

He clamps his eyes shut in the midst of his speech and

doesn't open them again.

"Destroying these..." he blindly gestures at the cluster of scorched birdhouses, "...artifacts is the least I can do to retaliate."

Red and blue lights appear in Gretchen's peripherals and she ducks behind some rhododendrons.

"Will I ever see you again?!" he shouts.

She emerges. A false alarm.

Unaware of Gretchen's preoccupations, the man enlists her help finding Tiffany, who may or may not have once lived there.

*

Their collusion is plumbed until it reaches a cavernous romance. Gretchen isn't sure if she's interested in Cole or interested in pirating his personality, however.

Cole had once survived a Cessna crash returning from a shark fishing expedition near Tampa Bay. He keeps a seat belt buckle from the flight as a talisman.

She tells him her name is Lacy because that sounds nice. She installs a two-way mirror between his bedroom and his closet.

Her thoughts spill out of doors one by one when he's there. His ideas supplant her previous realities. They begin to couple in exchange for each other's delusions.

Cole says to her, "I'll sit back and watch my fame spread throughout the world."

Gretchen's not sure what he's talking about but she confesses her severe case of pareidolia, or seeing faces in objects.

*

When he opens a package on his stoop, he uncovers a manual on hypnosis with the subtitle: *How to lure others into a trance state.*

He begins to suspect that Gretchen might not have true affections for him. Or perhaps she has a dangerous amount of true affections for him.

Gretchen summons Cole for her standard relationship questionnaire. She hands him the stack and he says, "This isn't the time or place. We haven't gotten anywhere with the Tiffany investigation."

He's not wrong, she admits.

*

Days later, he intercepts a package at her doorstep that reveals a human-size cage. Gretchen is digging in the ravine behind her house when it arrives.

"I guess I should do something about this," he says to the driveway.

He feels his eyelash attack its own eye.

They lunch in silence.

Clearing away the plates, Gretchen says, "Now is probably as good a time as any to close the investigation."

"What makes you say that?"

"We haven't made any progress."

"You haven't made any progress. But I have. She's settled outside of Indianapolis and my flight leaves in three hours."

"We'll see," Gretchen says, and Cole notices she's wearing his sweatpants.

CHAMBER NO. 5

A girl named Chelsea inspects what looks to be an old Easter basket on the porch. She doesn't know where it came from but wants to see if something will appear within it.

Less than a day later, she's not disappointed. She perches over it to extract a brochure glazed with the traditional promises of summer camp. Chelsea ferries the material inside and sets it atop her mother's placemat.

*

Gretchen's plan is working. The girl's exuberance for summer camp has fully absorbed, like no one had ever tampered with it.

She wants to hold space for the girl so that she can experience nurturing parents again. This Chelsea is an only child and her situation is rather cushy.

Gretchen is subbing for a teacher during the last week of school. She merely presses play on a series of movies each day.

She motions Chelsea over when the screen flickers with the tears that can only come from Old Yeller's demise.

"Did you hear about Camp Strongheart? Everyone's going this summer."

Chelsea nods.

"You know how you like to pretend to run away from home? This'll be sort of like that."

Gretchen places a mentorly hand on Chelsea's shoulder, then frowns and feels her face's tectonic plates shift into new wrinkles.

She continues, leaving the hand on the shoulder, "You're not a latchkey kid, are you?"

*

Five minutes after moving into the girl's bright bedroom, Gretchen understands the smugness behind Chelsea's permanent smirk.

She decides to write Chelsea a letter with her own stationery.

> Chels,
>
> Your parents have been very understanding about the substitute teacher exchange program. They agree that it might help kids empathize with subs more, and ultimately make the classroom environment more amenable for learning.
>
> You probably didn't know this but your house is haunted. The ghost follows me around. She doesn't seem to care about anyone else. Too bad no one can corroborate.
>
> While you are braiding friendship bracelets, your parents are letting me draw all over the walls with markers.
>
> While you are whittling sticks, they are smearing their cheeks with team colors in preparation for my swim meet. Your mother dabs puffy paint on poster board and your father fiddles with the old camcorder in order for us to compare notes on my freestyle afterwards.
>
> While you are dunking your sleeping bunk mate's hand in warm water, I am calling out my

own name in the meadow on the hill above your street.

Mrs. Newsome asked me what I wanted to be someday and when I told her a cartographer, she flushed and called me "remarkable."

Oh, and your mom requests makeovers constantly. I heat her hair into serpentine coils and dress her in chunky knit sweaters.

I can't tell you how good it feels that someone is obligated to attend to me.

Anyway—hope you're well.

Sincerely,
Gretchen

Despite all of these lies, Gretchen does encounter some facts during her stay.

Chelsea's father is a descendant of a Grand Master of the Chauffeurs, a French secret society filled with marauders.

Chelsea's mother is a personal injury lawyer, the kind who canopies herself across billboards, but everybody already knows that.

And since the father likes to leave news channels running, she also learns about a pack of escaped convicts hiding out somewhere in this very county. The pack's leader is named Romeo.

Gretchen wonders if they have an email address or perhaps a website. What if they could form a convict conglomerate? But if they cannot respond to inquiries, maybe her inquiries will be rescinded.

Mimicking a grade schooler is the only enterprise she currently has. Her mimicry is regressive in nature.

*

Gretchen's lantern crushes a packet of noodles at the bottom of her backpack as she traverses the forest.

She smells pine, leaf rot, and most importantly, smoke.

Darting across a creek, she practices her conversation skills.

"Once, for a whole week, every time I opened my mouth an alarm clock noise came out. My mouth was no longer reliable, it seemed."

She picks up the sound of twigs cracking over heat, some low murmuring.

Three figures loaf around a circle of flames up ahead.

They startle at the tinkling of her backpack's YKK zipper.

One stands.

"Is that you, Romeo?"

They run in different directions.

"Wait. Let me get situated," she shouts.

A Swiss Army knife lays irrevocably bent beside her feet. She curses them, then thinks she might have been the one who stepped on it.

CHAMBER NO. 6

———————

Gretchen is the first houseplant in history to win the lottery. The truth is, it wasn't the official lottery. She had found a roll of bills in a ditch. Money—sure, right when it's completely unnecessary.

A position had presented itself that weekend. A plant had withered and collapsed unexpectedly. She knew that she would slowly descend the stairs and take it upon herself to fill this position.

Besides, Chelsea is returning from camp.

The dead plant is some unknown species. Nothing like the local flora and fauna, she knows.

She grafts herself into place on the low shelf, unhindered by the trappings of humanity. The mother looks at her as if she expected this the whole time.

Nevertheless, Gretchen becomes the type of plant that gets transferred to the bathtub once per week for watering, along with the others. The mother is humoring her for some unknown reason.

She is left to drain.

As a plant, am I diluted or deluded, she wonders.

While the mother is at town council meetings and Chelsea is at practice, the father lumbers into different corners of the house and screams, seemingly for sport.

Meanwhile, Gretchen grows toward the light as only a houseplant can.

Imagine if she'd gone into high finance like her actual mother had once suggested. Gretchen is unyielding in whatever she devises. She requires and she composes and she lodges. She knows she craves an arrangement that's less like a relationship and more like a fistula.

Chelsea walks by and notices her for the first time.

"Feels flimsy to me," Chelsea says.

She ignores Gretchen for the remainder of her stay.

*

Nobody's home. Gretchen's hand, of its own accord, turns the basement doorknob.

She enters Chelsea's birthdate into the keypad and their family safe opens immediately.

Here, no doubt, their treasures accumulate.

Gretchen consults the dark square in front of her. There are estate planning papers, a map (that possibly leads to a bunker of gold doubloons—she wouldn't put it past them), a pile of indecipherable photographic negatives, and a human skull.

Running her hands along the smooth dome of bone, she nicks her finger. As the droplets cluster, she slams the safe closed and ventures to the bathroom.

Gretchen stares at the Band-Aid, still in its packaging, and addresses it, "You really must learn how to apply yourself."

The mother comes in from a jog around the block. Heaving tubercular breaths, she grasps her purse and water bottle to leave once again.

"Don't forget your coupons," Gretchen says from the shelf.

"This is getting out of hand."

"Alright. I can take my business elsewhere."

Gretchen cooperates by scooting down. Her landing is nearly graceful.

They've made it pretty clear they only approve of traditional existences. And you can only eat all the leftover pizza so many times before somebody sabotages your plans.

The mother collects Gretchen's briefcase from the hall closet. Gretchen pretends not to recognize it.

"What kind of operation are you running here?" the mother is asking but not really asking.

"I don't have to answer that."

Putting on her shoes by the door, Gretchen adds, "You're violating so many ordinances. You'll be fined soon enough."

Gretchen decides to breakfast at her favorite diner but stops at home first so she can bring her own cutlery.

CHAMBER NO. 7

She had to start with ditching her cell phone. Gretchen had connected a landline and absconded with her old friend Marleena's answering machine long ago.

She receives a message from a wrong number telling her to meet at a houseboat by the river tomorrow at nine. The voice doesn't specify whether that's A.M. or P.M. She plays the message over and over, repulsed.

The following day, she settles on a bench beside the river. There's only one boat. It's docked directly in view of the casino. It's not a houseboat. Not at all. Regardless, this must be the place, Gretchen deduces.

Hampered by the stranger's lack of specificity and not yet emboldened enough to track down her hunch, she decides that he meant nine at night, not nine in the morning like it is right now.

Gretchen doesn't go home. She continues to sit on the bench. She stares at a patch of dormant grass and tries not to think very deeply about its symbolism.

A breeze kicks up from the water. She puts her fingers on her neck to warm them, which feels like being mean and nice to herself at the same time. Maybe she is canceling herself out.

There's a doughnut cart over by the playground. She

stands down from her station for reinforcements and fraternizes with the pigeons by feeding them crumbs.

Finally, it's time. Gretchen enters what is meant to be the living room, bringing a wake of her own.

"The dockmaster must never see this," a man says from the ground.

He stops blinking away the blood from a gash on his forehead.

"You're still alive? I wasn't sure," Gretchen says.

"Tell it to the buoys."

According to the vinyl beside him, he wasn't the only victim. A mangled ball python lies on torn cushions.

"Can it be cured?" he asks, gesturing to the snake but not moving very much.

She wasn't sure if by "cured" he meant made into meat or healed. She doesn't answer.

There are so many ways to make it clear that a visitor doesn't belong, she thinks, and one of them is not using customary specifics when requesting said visitor in the first place, even if the message was intended for someone else. She could have arrived before it was too late. Still, she almost wishes she could decipher the architecture of helpfulness.

He looks like one giant and triumphant recessive gene, especially lying there on the floor like that. He probably studies escape routes of public buildings.

The man keeps shouting at her, "I keep shouting at you!"

But then he reaches a more suitable volume. He volunteers that he used to be a tightrope walker.

"How did you do it?" Gretchen asks.

"I could tell you, but it's much more interesting to learn how you do it," he says.

His small table holds what looks like a framed portrait of a slice of rhubarb pie.

"I used to think I wanted to be inconspicuous about my work. Like the daytime moon. Now I know I've always yearned to be caught. I can tell you're the same way. And yet you've failed me," he says, trying to get up.

Failing people. This is the sort of thing she can do.

"I know what you're getting at," she says.

The man seems to already know about her. She does want to be reprimanded, but the only people who notice her are the people who don't seem to mind.

"Look, there's a horde of angry civilians peering in the portholes and murmuring at us right now."

There isn't.

"Do you want...a Band-Aid?" she manages. "Or an MRI?" she tries again.

A woman joins them below deck and sets down her purse. Her name tag says: LUCKY.

"That student government your son is involved with, it's really just a puppet regime," Lucky says.

She sits down on the flayed cushions, right on top of the snake carcass, and unties her shoes.

CHAMBER NO. 8

She recognizes all the symptoms. The recurring dream has affixed itself to her subconscious again. Shaking it loose is always an undertaking.

In the dream, her favorite dead actor would beckon her into a duel, the results of which could fissure into a dozen outcomes, but flank her waking behaviors regardless.

Encumbered by a constant rustling, Gretchen plunges her hand into her pocket. A page she'd torn then harbored there during a visit to the public library ornaments her palm, though she has no recollection of doing it.

The page resounds with details of her favorite dead actor's lifestyle in the mid to late seventies, including the hotel where she took up residence in a corner suite.

Gretchen reads it like an itinerary.

*

The sun's vampiric leeching turns a billboard's giant onion rings into pallid and sickly advertisements to avoid the place altogether.

Her car's vents release a familiar wet-gravel smell.

She makes it into the lobby. The people in charge have been replaced by clipboards. A velvet curtain conceals the remainder of the front desk.

Gretchen awaits any kind of signal. She prowls near a table holding cookies, a water dispenser, fanned cocktail napkins, and equally fanned brochures that orbit the napkins.

A guest feigns interest in the brochures so he can embark on another cookie grab.

"Where's the hotel staff?" she asks.

But he doesn't hear her or pretends not to hear her.

Gretchen slaps her chest to gesture at an imaginary name tag. He startles.

"Are you having a heart attack? Do you need an ambulance?" he asks, panic morphing the chocolate-smeared corners of his mouth.

Someone emerges from behind the curtain.

Gretchen approaches the woman to request a corner suite.

"Does the room have a working fireplace? I have some items I need to incinerate."

The customer experience associate shakes her head and pushes a mini-folder of room keys across the counter.

On her floor, Gretchen demonstrates proper awareness of her surroundings by looking in the peepholes of every door.

One flies open while she's still leaning forward.

"Did you know the hotel gives you this little sign to hook onto your door handle that informs everyone when you do and do not want to be disturbed?" she tries.

The door is propped open with a foot. Her view ends with a shin bone.

"This must be very embarrassing for you," Gretchen says to the shin.

The door closes, capsizing her enthusiasm. She'd planned on asking all the guests where they were going.

Two double beds. What a waste. But maybe the actor had required such accommodations. She trusses up her memory with research to infiltrate the celebrity's psyche.

Yes, it's working. It's as if Gretchen has her tied up in the bathtub right now.

She turns to the shower curtain and says, "Start talking."

Getting into bed, she tucks the top of the flat sheet into her collar just like a napkin, ready to consume hours of sleep.

*

At breakfast, a TV anchored to the ceiling reports that the world's largest cave has its own ecosystem. Like that's hard to produce.

Another visitor approaches with a Belgian waffle. He sits at a table right next to her.

Gretchen swigs her orange juice and exhales.

"Things will never be different enough to be the same as they were," she says.

"Oh yeah?" asks the man.

His tongue lolls around syrupy morsels, revealing a tattoo of what looks to be an AK-47 atop his papillae.

"Definitely. Though my childhood was rather unmemorable, I guess."

"Tell me about it," he scootches closer.

"I was born at the edge of an animal rendering facility. Right beside the carcass compost bin. My mom worked as a fabricator for the metal snap manufacturing plant nearby. I come from a long line of fabricators."

Powdered eggs roil in her stomach. The stranger interprets it as past trauma resurfaced. He pats her shoulder.

"There now, was that so bad?" he says.

Gretchen twitches back into character.

"If you'll excuse me."

*

Last Saturday, a pack of dogs had followed her around town. Her dishes had been cultivating a sheath of dust from eating every meal over the sink. And look at her now.

Gretchen constructs a small platform in the lobby. She runs up to change clothes and produce a stack of glossy portraits.

Before she knows it, an autograph line rings the perimeter.

She cracks her knuckles and calls the first one over.

CHAMBER NO. 9

So it's time to acknowledge his head trauma, how much the wound gapes. Gretchen's windshield view from her reconnaissance van is nearly perfect.

She abandons her van and crests a slight incline toward the first crushed vehicle.

The injured man sways, reverberating like a human idiophone.

"I don't buy it," she says to him.

Then she recognizes this man as Mr. Schenley, the middle school science teacher.

He doesn't register her or anything else for that matter. Perhaps his brain is pickling itself under pressure.

"I'll take it from here," she says.

He only needs a gentle push westward and he's fording the ravine into the next town.

Passengers in the other car still haven't budged by the time the ambulance unspools from a newly developed line of vehicles.

"Ma'am, are you hurt?"

Gretchen covers her eyes like a necessary part of answering the question.

The crash began when the first driver glimpsed a two-headed turtle skulk into the right lane.

Distant bystanders reconstruct the scene. One claims Mr. Schenley perpetrated the whole thing, that he was a drunk and everybody knew it. Another reports that the two were in the midst of a zesty drag race.

Nobody mentions a woman grafting herself into the accident.

Poor Mr. Schenley has become as stymied as his living conditions, Gretchen thinks, if he really does live in his classroom like all the students suspect.

Turns out he lives on an actual ranch with some livestock. His property rests enfolded in endless rows of traditional ranch houses. Like a developer heard the word "ranch" and started construction without looking around. A prairied belly button sullies the gerrymandered map of residential streets. For him, home is pasture and order and control. But they won't know any of this until they read the paper the following week.

Gretchen is plunged into an ambulance and taken to the hospital.

Before she's fully examined, they put her in a spacious single room.

She can't be bothered to lie very well—only lie still—so she knows her stay will end soon.

A nurse enters.

"This wall could use a trompe l'oeil of some kind. Maybe a Magic Eye poster. Yeah," Gretchen weakly signals.

If she had to, she could always hide sandwiches under her bed.

But a security guard arrives instead.

Gretchen is picked up, carried out of the room, and placed onto the curb.

She walks downtown to consult the drained fountain.

Scanning her surroundings, she catalogues: some street with a name she always forgets, some building with windows and probably a door, some truck that some person parked there for some reason.

This atmosphere benights her with a plan. She returns home brandishing the unapologetic exuberance of a man putting his cap back on while leaving the barbershop.

*

Gretchen's mail-order bride arrives faster than expected.

When the cops finally trouble themselves with Gretchen's capture, she'll try to be tucked into a stately manor as a quaint newlywed named Salome.

First, the real Salome must be educated. She has her fill out a guest book under the guise of mail-order company training. Their cultures emulsify over afternoon tea parties. You wouldn't be able to cut the tension with a knife.

Still, they have their spats.

"Don't make me regret this. Your future husband is waiting for you to pass our course," she tells her.

At night, Gretchen plants her ear to their shared wall and listens to Salome talk to herself.

They traipse down aisles at the grocery store. Gretchen follows Salome around with a notebook. Salome chooses a cereal box and sets it in their cart with a slight twitch.

"What will you do with that?"

"Eat it?" she tries.

"Be more specific."

Salome rocks her shoe against a wheel of their cart until it whines.

Gretchen scribbles hard. She stares back at an old lady with dented cans in both hands.

Inside her notebook, she's taped local classified ads and printed Craigslist posts of those desperately hunting for spouses.

CHAMBER NO. 10

_____

"Fruit salad! Fruit salad!" shouts Salome from the floor.

Gretchen startles, waking up from a dream about that very dish. She wonders who influenced who. Then she wonders why Salome is lying on the ground beside her bed.

This display is one in a pageant of questionable maneuvers by the mail-order bride. Yesterday, they'd gone to the mall to get Salome's ears pierced.

"You won't feel a thing," Gretchen had said to her.

But she never flinched.

"You must have permanent accessories," Gretchen had continued, "Men like that. We'll get you a cane later."

Plus, Gretchen has been compiling a dossier on the most promising suitor, leaving it out on the kitchen table every night, but every morning it sits unexcavated.

Leroy, a real estate agent, had listed himself like a mid-century ranch. Before she knows it, Gretchen will be a person with car keys, credit cards, a signature. She will be at large.

*

Conducting a test on Salome's developments in household management, she finds Salome running two loads at once, dryer balls acting as the timpani of her laundry orchestra.

Another task Gretchen will soon unlearn once she convinces Leroy it's time for a maid. She will be unhampered by hampers and boasting an abundance of credible backstory.

Gretchen tallies the wash score and carries on to Salome's room. All of her suitcases lay entangled, open and lacking belongings.

To slake her doubts, she circles back to Salome, who is now measuring the living room furniture.

"I've seen enough."

Salome drops the tape.

"You aren't the least bit curious about your suitor? You don't want his particulars?"

Salome shrugs.

"I guess you don't have to go through with it. We could find you a way out. There's a guy who'd lease you a room in a houseboat. You'll have to start baking because he only accepts payment in the form of pie. But there's an element of physical danger involved if you go that route."

Salome turns away and roams the kitchen.

In a voice Gretchen doesn't recognize, Salome says, "Ever since I can remember I've wanted to wile away your remaining lifespan. I've made it my life's work."

"But we just met like a week and a half ago," Gretchen says.

"Yet here we are," she smiles, still talking in the new voice.

Gretchen tries to collect herself. There's no reason to get upset. Salome has somehow figured out her plan but is willing to go along with it.

So she picks up the phone. As it's ringing, Gretchen glances at the TV. A priest hovers over a hotel sink on the screen. He stretches out his hand toward a small box labeled VANITY KIT, then pulls it back.

"Hit me," the phone says.

"Uh, Betsy? Is it you?" Gretchen asks.

"That's right," Betsy says.

"This is Gretchen. You know, Marleena's friend. The badminton player."

"I thought you were dead."

"Not yet. Listen, I'm calling to invite you to a going away party...for a friend. It's tomorrow. You can drop by anytime.

"I hear ya," Betsy says while hanging up.

Salome invites her favorite bagger from the grocery store. Gretchen hears the name and instantly forgets it.

*

Besty pulls up to Gretchen's house and opens the backseat to release Atom the groundhog. She gets back in and peels out.

On the patio, Salome, Gretchen, and the bagger take turns throwing candy at a pinata filled with sticks.

Gretchen wants to wait until the album ends or the speaker battery dies to announce Salome's supposed destiny. She thinks it'll add dramatic weight, like her statement stopped time.

Salome gorges on chips out of boredom, just as her parents did, and their parents before them.

Nacho cheese oozes out into space and lands in her lap, making a mess of her pants and eventually the rest of her life.

Gretchen passes her a napkin using whatever stands in for concern.

Traipsing over to Atom, she hears the bagger ask Salome, "Why does she always walk like that?"

Gretchen is tempted to wait and hear the answer but must retrieve her groundhog before he encounters a dog next door.

The music stops.

"Well, I guess this is where we say goodbye," Gretchen says, too flustered to begin her prepared speech.

"I guess so," Salome agrees, patting Gretchen on the back with increasing strength and speed.

They push each other into the road. They take turns staring. The bagger starts directing traffic around them.

STORIES

She kept at her meat.
　　　　—Diane Williams

KEEL

_____

Let's say we're all summoned to our uncle's house to figure out who gets what in his estate. Nothing special, really. We're called to the drawing room by Nico, his lawyer or executor or whoever, but the drawing room is really a corner of the garage.

This summoning yields a fraction of the funeral attendees. Rows and rows of acquaintances had just finished swallowing their ancient resentments in a dim sanctuary.

Some of us are taking our sweet time getting here. One is forced to wait for a train to pass. One of us is here but keeps proposing to another one's wife and it's getting uncomfortable. And one of us materializes in the nude saying, "I wish you would concern yourselves with me."

The most responsible of us was tasked with spreading our uncle's ashes in the drive-through line of the Dunkin' Donuts, as requested. He'd completed the task already, and with a Styrofoam coffee cup in hand, starts pestering another sitting atop a stationary bike in the garage. He's pretending it's a normal bike that's broken.

"Looks like you're stuck. Do you need a hand," he says.

Someone rummages in bathroom drawers to figure out what brand of deodorant the old guy used.

Nico sips from his personal two-liter. The bottle pops under its own pressure. We take to the sound like a dinner bell.

He reads us a message from beyond the grave. Through Nico, our uncle tells us, "I'm dead, you big sickos, and it's just the way I imagined it."

A scoff punctuates this statement. The one hunkered in the bathroom has closed the door and is doing who knows what, but is still listening, we guess.

"Let's cut to the chase," he says from behind the door. "Who gets the monkey?"

The People's Liberation Army of China enlisted macaque monkeys to prevent birds from taking down military aircraft. They were real-life monkey commandos. And somehow our uncle had retrieved one.

"The monkey commando is the only reason we showed up," our stationary bike correspondent shouts.

Nico continues reading aloud.

"From time immemorial, you all have coveted my garbage, you know that. I have codified this will and testament so that only the most qualified family members will get the goods. For starters, remember that time Denise removed a kidney of mine in the beverage aisle of the gas station down the street? Well, I jarred that sucker. And Peter deserves my jarred kidney."

Peter looks up, shakes his head, and backs into some fishing poles hung against the wall.

"No? You sure? In that case, I'd like to buy it from you," says Nico, through what we estimate is his actual personhood rather than the will-reading-automaton version.

Nico picks up where he left off.

"It's not that Elaine has earned my esteemed ship in a bottle, but she'll at least dust it regularly, unlike the rest of you."

He hands her the ship in a bottle, which appears to glow in her hands.

"Nobody will hold it against you if you hold it against you," he says, and this time we can't tell who's really speaking.

"Don't gloat, okay? Something's seriously wrong with your bike. You haven't gotten anywhere. And you heard what he said. You shouldn't even be getting this thing in the first place. I know about that time. The time a stranger kept insisting he lived in your college dorm room so you caved and let him have it? Yeah," says one of us.

"That was me," says the bathroom door.

Nico's face looks more and more porous with each second we're here.

"In theory, deceased people have no use for land. And so with this great rigamarole presented to you in the confines of my quaint drawing room, I bequeath my countryside property to Marie."

"You mean the giant sinkhole? She can have it."

"My beloved family, don't make me rescind any of these valuables from your grasp. Their powers may overwhelm you. So I leave you with a question only you can answer: If a group of clowns gather in a room, does that make it a circus?"

Nico compiles a few papers.

"Wait, that's it?!"

"What about the monkey commando? Or even this house?"

One of us grabs the ship in a bottle and smashes it onto the floor. That one has always been especially good at smashing.

"Let me explain," the smasher says. He picks up what looks to be the ship's keel. "There's...minimal damage."

"The commando has been claimed," Nico says.

"Cough up the monkey! Where is it?"

"Elsewhere," he says.

Then we all start smashing things. The garage is full of smashable items. There's a whole movement that begins, right here in this garage. We exhaust ourselves with the smashing and before we know it we're asleep.

Nico leaves while we're still passed out.

The one waiting for the train to pass stumbles in.

"It's 10 P.M. Do you know where your Hot Pockets are," she says to a somnambulant crowd.

She'd detoured into a bar earlier because she didn't know how to deal with what she'd witnessed.

"You guys. Guys. I think I saw a monkey hopping a train. Just like a vagabond. Like the—the Boxcar Children," she says.

We ignore her, same as always.

YOU CAN RENEW
YOUR VOWS AT
CHUCK E. CHEESE
ANYTIME YOU LIKE

There they are attempting hand-to-hand combat in an automobile. Imagine their surprise once they run out of breath.

"And I was going to pluck out your fingernail! And you were reaching for a pressure point!"

They had mostly just garnished each other with matching tricep bruises.

These two detectives can't untangle the impetus of their physical froth, but one of them can recall hearing something to the effect of, "You think you can just walk into my life and host a picnic?"

One had watched a vendetta-style movie with his wife last night. His reflex to enact justice was freshly fueled from the viewing while his wife came away from it feeling like she already had.

These two are accustomed to itineraries, formalities. Now, a lip is bleeding and a knee joint crackles.

"Guess I'm not president of the thumb wrestling club for nothing," one says as a sort of conclusion.

The street is becoming more and more populated as they idle outside the basket shop.

Earlier that morning, they had received a tip leading them across town. There was a man-made lake where an office park was supposed to be.

Everybody knows that this basket shop is managed by a cult. That's how it's always operated. In this town, baskets are startlingly dangerous.

Citizens here sure do extract heaps of joy from picnicking. There's a coveted spot under the tree in front of the lumberyard's main entrance. Many appreciate this tree's beckoning defiance beside such an establishment.

But the shop itself leaves most with a sense of pageantry imitating hospitality. Regardless, sporting a picnic basket from anywhere else proves unsuitable.

The shop owner had dispersed the rumor about herself: she was a shrewd cult leader not to be crossed.

Since the age of five, she had run away from home every year, extending into adulthood. However, in order to keep leaving, she must keep returning, which deflates a fraction of its power.

Upon meeting her, she almost always defaults to saying, "The picnic business. It's no picnic," irrespective of whether it comes up in conversation.

She also whispers to every patron that she's training a chimp to answer her correspondence. She claims to be in various stages of experimentation. A primate has yet to emerge. How this figures into her cult no one can really say.

These detectives will catch her amid some illegal practice, that is certain. Once they draw her out, though, they don't know what they'll do with her.

The store employees—her supposed followers—are hushed dirigibles grasping price sticker guns. And the picnic crowd is so unhelpful it seems in league with the staff.

The detectives have not found life easy or breezy as a result.

"My husband came with nine trench coats," says one of their wives at every cocktail party.

Fogged with the question of what it takes for someone's words to be said once and continue to play in your mind versus someone who repeats the same phrase on a regular basis that you ignore, but also fogged with the very real condensation from their scuffle, the detective sitting in the driver's seat reviews his notes.

The other exits the vehicle to find some gauze. His mother and a stranger stand on the corner looking at him.

His partner watches from the car and notes that he asks the stranger for assistance rather than his mother.

Neither of them can equip him with what he needs, so he turns back.

The one inside tries to hide his notebook a bit too late.

"Why would you write that about my mother?"

"I believe it's integral to the case."

The car's windows start clouding over again, so to avoid another incident, one says, "Listen, I'm sorry about what happened. I think we can both agree that I'm a passionate person."

"Thank you. I'm sorry too. I didn't mean it. You can renew your vows at Chuck E. Cheese anytime you like."

Chapped with whether or not they are actually apologizing or trying to add in last-minute insults, they find that the picnic cult isn't what matters now.

And why should they tell you if it ever matters again.

DREDGE

Diane returns home from work to find their neighbor Lee depositing a slip of paper in their mailbox.

When she opens the car door, he offers her a saltine.

"No, thank you. I'm fasting for a medical procedure."

"It's okay. I rubbed all the salt off."

She declines again, wading over to the mailbox.

Lee's note reads:

> *Please allow us to continue using your pool despite the fact that you've turned into a dinosaur-shaped chicken nugget.*
> *Sincerely,*
> *Lee*

"What's this all about?" she asks.

"Hey, are you planning on doing anything with that?" He gestures toward her husband's SUV.

Diane reminds herself that Lee once superglued a Bentley hood ornament on his bicycle.

Phil walks out and aligns himself with the treed perimeter.

To Phil, Lee's hands look larger all of a sudden, like they could grasp and dunk with ease.

Lee advances toward him.

"Here, use this."

He hands Phil an excuse from the local school nurse.

*

Phil goes about the business of being a dinosaur-shaped chicken nugget.

Their son Blake brings home a foreign exchange student from a country Blake's never heard of. He doesn't remember the student's name either so he calls her Marcy.

They've avoided serving poultry at dinner since Phil's identity crisis in order to keep a convivial atmosphere, but everyone's tired of pork chops.

"Pass me the chops. And the peas. And the potatoes. I want it all," Blake says.

"I want it all," he repeats. "It's the American way."

He looks at "Marcy" to ensure she's paying attention.

They air the news: this year's prom queen tossed her tiara in the lake. She then rented some expensive equipment to immediately dredge the lake. But the tiara was reduced to pond scum and chipped plastic like an unforgiving friend.

"I'm done with tiaras. Being done with things: it's the American way," Blake says.

*

Since dinosaur-shaped chicken nuggets don't seem to wash the dishes or fold the laundry, they bring in a mediator.

His KEEP CALM & DRINK COFFEE mug—filled with an iced liquid—sweats down its sides.

Phil can already tell the mediator is speeding toward platitudes. He barters with a confession to get out in front of it.

"I'll be the first to admit I wish I had turned into something else. Like Tupperware. Then I could be the container instead of the contained."

"You see now what am I supposed to do with statements

like that?" There is a howl inside Diane's inquiry.

The mediator situates photocopies of song lyrics in front of them without remark. They ignore them.

"I know what this is about. You've wanted to go live in the treehouse ever since you installed it."

Phil thinks she's halfway right. Though he prefers a theater loge for optimal heckling. He spies the mediator's notebook page filled with 3D cubes and diamond-shaped Ss.

"Rescue your value from the mailer's BOGO pages before the garbage truck delivers it to a new kind of soiled auditor," mopes Diane.

Phil places their papers on the mediator's lap and says, "Our photocopying days are over."

"But I was the one who made these photocopies," he says to their backs.

Late afternoon introduces the dinosaur-shaped chicken nugget and its wife to another visit from the exchange student. Somehow "Marcy" has been impaled by a mechanical pencil.

"Let's make good use out of your wound by turning it into a bud vase. Resourcefulness. This too is the American way," says Blake.

He leans in, then turns away.

"You are now the landing pad for my vomit helicopter."

Blake and "Marcy" leave to observe the erecting of a new statue in town. A firefighter resting on a couch is cast in stone.

Upon Blake's return, they reinstate a formerly abandoned family meeting. A conclusion crusts itself over their itinerary.

They move into a grocery store where Phil can feel more comfortable.

Blake takes to initialing each item in the store, convincing customers that they're wheeling around collectors' items in their carts.

EMPTY GESTURES

———————

You can find a life cheerleader on the internet no problem. This is different than a life coach. There's little to no coaching involved; someone simply affirms you and everything you stand for. Standing is key. My hand-me-down table can stand by itself unsupported, and who's to say that can't be me someday?

The more enthused this person will get the more subdued and laidback I can finally become. And I got over embarrassment a long time ago.

The service is a fairly new operation, but there's no horseplay involved. I can be somewhat first on the scene, like a lookout.

There are plenty of male life cheerleaders—even a few trained dogs—but mine turns out to be female. Her name is Betsy.

I offer her a juicebox and a plate of fish sticks when she arrives.

"Thanks for being here, Betsy."

"Somebody has to."

She lodges herself in my papasan chair.

"The world should know that I exist. Your recognition will go a long way."

"Yes. I'm a friend of sorts," she says.

On general principle, I don't allow anyone to enter my apartment. Never! I wonder if Betsy can detect it. She wilts across the rattan frame's self-rotating axis.

"I'd like to switch things up in my career. Dive into trades from-of-old. Study shipbuilding even. Do you have any contacts in the shipbuilding community?"

"That's not how this works."

My right hand goes numb for no reason. I shake out my fingers and wait for gravity to catch up.

"Or I could go a different route. I hear there's a position called 'pain specialist.' That sounds fitting with my experience."

Is Betsy undercover? Does she have assorted costumes? Can she maneuver in the stealthiest of circles? Who can tell?

"I'm really just getting started here. I've always wanted to pursue this humanitarian effort, for instance. You know Race for the Cure? I'd do that, but it's for the band. The Cure. They've had too many people come and go from the lineup. They need our help."

You start with the music. And then—the world. But I keep that to myself. The plan's too powerful. It's not ready to be unleashed just yet.

"Sounds great," Betsy says, but I can tell she doesn't mean it.

"I monitor the band members. Here and there. I thought I'd be running a bar at this point, but that's out the window."

"Hmm."

"No, literally, it's out the window. Someone chucked the bar top out through the second story panes. What a nightmare."

The truth is my dad owned that bar. And Betsy knows it.

So this is what all those married people are going on about. Someone to corroborate your story. My life cheerleader stays around for much longer than I expected. She comes over every Tuesday. Tuesdays with Betsy. That's the cheerleading package I can afford.

"I'm eating these but you still can't," I wave a bowl of prehistoric tater tots in her face.

"Fantastic," she says.

"You can have one of those bananas over there. I'm not gonna. They're not worth the banana thumb."

Betsy nods, then says, "Huh?"

"Banana thumb. You know, the little black line that forms under your thumbnail after you peel it. My nails are short. Can't pick it out. Gets stuck all day. Not worth the peel."

"Then why do you buy them?"

"You're the cheerleader," I say. "You tell me."

This is no time for her to loaf. Word has gotten around.

In the surveillance footage, you can see my tattoo of Cure frontman Robert Smith peeking out from underneath my collar right as I'm charging lacquered wood through glass. People freeze but eventually start grabbing bottles off the shelves and privately chugging them.

My dad'll never speak to me again, probably.

Betsy pats my shoulder with one hand and feeds herself a banana with the other.

"Like you mean it," I say.

She starts smacking. Then she carries me out the door. We find her car. She gives me a piggyback ride through the forest and sets me down at the mouth of a cave.

I sit among the troglobites and guano. I consider aging cheeses in here.

My echo reassures me that'd be a wise move.

LET THE
GROUNDHOG DO
THE TALKING

There is no other way to say this: my sister has the face of a kidnapper. She even owns a house with the ideal cellar for hostages.

In her attempts to bring forth the inner nature that accompanies her outer visage, she has altogether failed. She meted out her escapades of tailing vehicles and observing strangers in the midst of mundane inanities and yet it still unraveled before it really began.

To recover from not being a kidnapper, she joined a biker gang. It turned out that most of them didn't believe in gravity, however, and she didn't have the sensibilities for that type of operation.

So she took to training her dog. He can do just about anything now. And this sates her, at least somewhat.

I'm nesting in a couch corner while she's designating shelf space for her groceries.

A man materializes in the corridor between us.

"You were there," he says, gesturing toward my sister, "in the ball pit."

She disregards his claims by continuing to unload her bags on the counter.

"Don't you feel beholden to me?" he asks, unconcerned with his intrusion.

I encrust myself on the cushions, completely immobile. If only she wouldn't have trained the dog to unlock doors, I manage to think.

He walks closer to her and nudges a box on the counter.

"We're not here to talk about your radicalized cereals. We made a deal," he says, pointing out the window.

We look out to find a van with an oversized loudspeaker atop its roof parked crookedly along the curb.

"We've never met and I don't know what you're talking about, but you expect me to drop everything and get in that van with you, don't you?" she asks.

He nods.

"Let's," she says.

*

The van squad is composed of who we now call Ira, my sister, and me. Sometimes her recently retired neighbor tags along too.

I agreed to be in the van squad.

Yeah, I agreed to be in the van squad.

I'm not saying I'm too good for it. But I have to get out of a situation and this is a decent place to lay low, if you can believe it. Ira squires us through traffic like nobody's business.

We are a squad today, but who knows, one day we might be a regime.

Honestly, I'm not too good for much. I eat a single chip in multiple bites. I vigorously rub my hands together at all the wrong moments.

We primarily chug down residential streets, wailing our grievances into the loudspeaker as we go. That's our main mission, according to Ira.

As if the van weren't enough, we're also supplied with walkie-talkies.

We scatter truth and double-A batteries left and right.

*

"Hey, look, an actual mall rat."

This is what happens when your freedom of speech shatters every noise ordinance in the tri-county area. We overtake the abandoned shopping mall, constructed in some decade or other, as our hideout.

"Are you wearing your bulletproof vest?" Ira asks my sister.

She doesn't respond.

He turns to her neighbor, who happens to be with us.

"Start digging outside. Gather a core sample. We may need to take things underground."

Ira hands the man a shovel and a test tube. He makes the face we all do when Ira starts stipulating.

The reasons why we're here stop being clear to us when Ira plans to establish the second most famous groundhog in the world. He seems to be getting off track, losing focus.

"Let the groundhog do the talking," he chants.

Meanwhile, our loudspeaker lamentations enter the dreams of the citizenry. They unite in thoughts, moods, imaginings. We are tampering with the collective unconscious. We are grafting in our own notions and rooting down a false peace.

BEST AVAILABLE HUMAN

———————————

"You've been looking for a way in for so long. And here it is."

Have I?

"But this isn't really how I operate," I say.

My mother had arranged a meeting with my fake uncle. He's someone my parents knew in college.

"You have a lot of potential and nothing else to go with it," my mother argues.

"What is he doing with himself these days anyway?" I ask.

"I've heard several versions and only one of them seems trustworthy."

She doesn't elaborate.

"Listen, he is capable," she says. "Instead of 'no,' he says things like, 'It doesn't work out that way conceptually.'"

One or both of us loses interest in the conversation.

*

I manipulate myself into a chair up against a corner of the restaurant and await my companion.

He is a wallet with a man attached. We embark on this encounter as if we thought of it ourselves.

He insists on administering a presentation but keeps calling it an instructional video. His laptop wheezes beside our cutlery.

The first slide reads: MAKING THE BIG SALE.

"Are you thinking about nachos?" I ask.

He ignores me, foraging for the right key to press.

"Recently, I sent my diaries over to a foundation that requested them, so this doesn't reflect my entire legacy," he says.

He maneuvers the next slide in place. Its text whooshes in from the left-hand side, which reads: MEDICAL MARVEL.

"An accomplished yodeler spent years studying my larynx."

A server surfaces at that moment and he accidentally says this while staring right into her eyes. She collects some crumbs and keeps moving.

Our tablecloth matches the texture of his pride—knotted and bulbous linen lying flush against particleboard.

"Let's talk about assets," he continues. "I once dated a movie star who owned three Bengal tigers. When she ultimately overdosed and died, I found out she had bequeathed said tigers to me."

I slice more roast beef and think it tastes like the hot pink light they place it under.

Then my fake uncle kills the screen and says, "I once made a troublesome pizza delivery guy disappear."

He takes a call yet still musters a reply, pointing at me and walking away, saying, "Good luck trying to pin me on that one."

When he returns I say, "I'm one of those troublesome pizza delivery guys you hear about."

I articulate the point by strangling my own neck, my tongue a pendulum for emphasis.

"Kidding. I'm really the town guru."

I fling a fry off my plate, lean in, and pretend to whisper,

"I've seen more spectacles than a YMCA locker. You name it."

Not wanting to leave any room for oneupmanship, I add while getting up to find the bathroom, "I convinced a nudist colony to start wearing socks. They're still totally naked otherwise. You should see them now."

I rap on the adjacent stall and receive the corresponding knocks back.

"I came in as soon as I got your French fry," the stall says.

"You have to admit, the guy has some gumption."

"Then why are we here if you're so impressed?" asks the stall.

"No more for me," I reply.

The night is over, a sham.

"Fine."

I hear my best friend's boots squawk away and out the door. They have lots of tread which can sound like the opposite of intimidation on certain floors. We have a secret oath, and covering for each other like this is part of it. She is the best available human.

I flush and wash vigorously while staring at the "Employees must wash hands" sign.

We assemble back at the table.

"This is my associate," I say. "Something came up."

Dara takes my seat.

I watch the scene through the restaurant window. When I put my hands in my pockets, I pull out a deranged fork.

Did I steal this? I'm trying not to think things anymore. It's my fork now.

The two of them are laughing. They have their palms clutching their respective chests as a sign of overwhelming amusement.

But my fake uncle presses his hand against his chest a little too long. He starts smacking with it and slumping over. He's choking or having a heart attack, I'm sure.

I abandon my post before I can gather more details.
Am I on the run?
I jaywalk while chainsaws harmonize in the distance.

LET'S SEE THAT AGAIN

We're splitting a sandwich named after him at the deli when he strolls in. The sandwich is wrapped up in such a way as to resemble a wet fist.

He's our less-famous version of a famous person. We call him The Mayor, though he's not into politics. He has a homemade key to the city and everything. He's what you might call a sensation.

We're here under the auspices of lunch.

He injects himself into a booth like only The Mayor knows how. He's not trying to cause a commotion, but he doesn't want to remain indistinguishable from the other sandwich-eaters either. We motion him over. He cooperates.

Here's the ugly truth: we trust the guy.

The Mayor squinches across vinyl to join us at our table.

"The fact is, we need your help. We received this yesterday."

We nudge the package toward him but it's like he doesn't see it or maybe it's underwhelming to him.

After about three seconds, he budges. As he reaches for the package, a pepper shaker tumbles.

"Let's see that again," we say in unison, practicing our

best sports announcer voices.

This is a habit we've adopted of late: creating fake sports replays of mundane blunders.

The Mayor looks at us, seemingly unperturbed. He opens the package to find a bubble-wrapped Tupperware container filled with leftovers and a few T-ball participation ribbons scattered around it.

"You know what this means?" one of us asks.

He closes his eyes, summoning a prescient response. We stop him before he can guess wrong.

"Our son has run away with his old babysitter. He left this for us on the kitchen counter."

Margie. She was a dutiful babysitter back in the 90s.

She still has her charms, yes. She's renowned for her casseroles. She confiscates nonrecyclable items from everyone's recycling bins and burns them in an open subdivision lot.

"Listen, I've seen sons turn to unknowably dire circumstances," says The Mayor. "Believe you me, this is nothing."

Our son is an adult. There's not much we can do, really.

"Don't pay it any mind," he continues. "I'll look into it."

"We were hoping that your son could—"

"—Right. You don't need to wire a place when your slapshod apartments share a wall. I'll talk to him."

We feel less confident about The Mayor's son. Not doomed per se. We watched him saw off the head of a roadkill deer to mount on his game room wall a few years back. At his auto repair shop, he only takes cash. You can never hand it to him directly. You have to place it between the teeth of his pitbull, square in the mouth. Then the pitbull takes it to the back office. That rule goes for everybody. And his father is no exception.

"We appreciate it."

"Don't worry about it. Plenty more where that came from."

He slides out of the booth.

*

The Mayor arranges a meeting at a chain restaurant of yore the following week. The meeting is a bust; we can see that right away.

Here we were each thinking, *This is my moment*, and a few seconds later we're in the thick of it, flustered as all get-out.

For one thing, The Mayor's son doesn't even show up. His girlfriend arrives twenty minutes late.

"Thanks for meeting us here. We're hoping you can corroborate the story we've pieced together about our son."

"Who?" she says.

The way she said it—how can we put this—it's like she was smacking gum even though she wasn't.

"Our son who ran away. With Margie, we think. Didn't The Mayor brief you on this?"

"Lost interest," she says, refusing to look at us.

We pivot.

"How do you make a living again? What's your career? The Mayor said it was rather impressive."

"Computer stuff," she says.

"What did you hear between the wall? This is where you come in. This is where you're supposed to come in."

It doesn't matter which one of us is speaking because we're thinking the same things. About her, about the whole charade.

"Make me," she says.

But that's not the rough part.

She starts up with, "You know what you should be doing right now? You should be, at this juncture, taking notes. Of what I'm saying, who's coming through the door, the grams of fiber listed on your cereal box, everything."

"But you've refused to tell us anything."

A waiter approaches.

"Excuse me," the girlfriend says, "That lady over there, she—well, at least someone who looks like a woman—she told me that we can get half-price drinks and apps right now. Does that include the—" she snaps her fingers when the waiter looks away, "—Yes, hello. Does that include the mozzarella sticks?"

He nods and solemnly takes our orders.

"Boy, they don't get PhDs in kindness here, do they?" she says.

Her point is made. And yet she hasn't made a single point.

Which brings us to three months from now, when our grocer will conjure a witness. A kid trying her first cigarette on the rooftop of a boutique had seen our son clasping hands with Margie. The two of them had shimmied into the backseat of an unidentified Prius, presumably a ride sharing vehicle, and rode away from town.

Turns out we didn't need this witness because we got a postcard from them the next day. GREETINGS FROM KANSAS, the front read. *We're not at home anymore*, the back read. In poor penmanship, we might add.

AMONG OTHERS

We draw up plans to convene on the usual premises. Last time, we cooperated enough to produce a confessional dinner party handbook—the only one in the region, or the world, probably.

All the meat is cut on a bias. Serrated knives are hidden away as a precaution. Specialty napkins and courtesy pillows flank each seat at the long table. Gentle sprays of vaguely vegetal arrangements lure the most reticent among us.

Our host answers the door like she was waiting directly behind it. She was born with six fingers on each hand. When she waves hello or goodbye, you feel she really means it.

But when she greeted me I thought I'd arrived at the wrong house. I couldn't identify her for a solid three minutes. That is until I looked down to find her fingers carousing with the average number of accomplices. Five on each side.

She shows me her latest acquisition while I struggle to acclimate: a burgundy velvet robe with gold trim. Embroidered across the right breast in a clean script is the name ELVIS.

"I scavenged through a Memphis consignment shop. What do you think?"

Still girdled by disorientation, I hesitate before shouting, "Who can really tell the difference between one Elvis and another?"

She slips it on and adjusts its belt before welcoming more guests.

Here in these headquarters, we intrude upon one another's lives to decipher brutal and untellable secrets.

"I'll start," our host says.

We suspend our forks and wine glasses midair, awaiting her confession.

"After the surgery, I saw my therapist. It was our regularly scheduled appointment. The same one we've held for close to a decade. But when I arrived, they sat me down and had me complete all this new patient paperwork. They didn't know who I was. Because of my hands. Can you believe that?"

They laugh. I tongue a beef hunk lodged in the back corner of my mouth. Almost seems deliberate, her choosing this story. Like she could read me as I crossed the threshold. Why did she remove the most interesting appendages she owned anyway? Surgery should be reserved for the innumerable ways the body sabotages itself. The landmines we call moles, for example.

I start laughing just as everyone has quieted down. I place myself in circulation.

"Something's happened to me." I blink. I say, "Forget it." But I don't really mean it.

They all nudge me.

"I kept spotting what looked like the same squirrel in my backyard. Who can really be sure though, right? So I made, uh, I fashioned this little cowboy hat for it in order to tell it apart. The hat has one of those elastic straps so it stays on."

I look around to gather their facial expressions.

"There," I say in relief.

"Oh, you won't believe mine. It's too wild," another starts.

They all laugh again, I presume anticipatorily.

"Let's put it this way: I've become obsessed with Bath & Body Works. The old mall still has one. I don't know what it is. I guess I never recovered once they launched their Cucumber Melon line. And I've been suppressing it for years until the past couple of months. I used to dress in disguise but gave up after the first couple times. They put me under surveillance. A mall cop took me down to the basement to question me."

That was nothing. I'd gotten myself into worse. I belong in mall basements.

Another pretty lame one comes through. A guest has been rummaging through other people's belongings, enamored with the possibilities of private lives established elsewhere.

Someone else pipes up, says, "You know how I vacationed in Fiji over Christmas? Well, most of you know that. While I was there, I started taking these long walks on the beach early in the morning, as one does. Nobody was out there before 6:00 except a handful of fishing boats aways offshore. On my last morning there, this guy emerges from some seagrass or bushes or whatever. He's visibly dirty and his hair and clothes are all ragged. Says he's shipwrecked, could I help him, which I know right away is a dumb lie. Who gets shipwrecked these days? I ask him if he's really shipwrecked, where's his vessel? But he starts moaning. He won't stop. Guy sounds like a whale. Then he goes like catatonic on me. I figure he's dead and start digging a nice burial plot for him right there along the beach. Just when I've dug a pretty sizable hole, some lady in this atrocious bathing suit—the kind with the built-in skirt?—comes out, scoops him up in her arms, and carries him to the closest resort. My muscles are still sore from all that digging."

Long before a food fight and light arson tarnish the

scene, I leave. If it wasn't clear before this, I don't like any of these people.

I run a red light on the way home, feeling a bump against the undercarriage simultaneously.

When I get a traffic violation letter in the mail a few weeks later, I study the accompanying photograph. Barely discernible in its pixelated pedantry, I see a shadow under my right-front tire. The shadow is squirrel-shaped, but different. What can only be a custom-made cowboy hat smothers its tiny rodent face.

I frame the photo and position it on my bedside table. This squirrel isn't going anywhere.

FEED US TO THE SWANS

Because now they are being interrogated, five hours after breaking and entering, six hours after deciding to break-and-enter, and one day after receiving an eviction notice, all she wants to do is tell the truth.

She trespasses. She does so whenever she can.

It doesn't take long for a froth of confession to cultivate in her throat, lashing her organs and xylophoning her ribs.

The thing that concerns her the most: how willing she is to talk. How unfazed she can be. And just how navigable the situation appears.

"This car was creeping down the road, going 29 right in front of me. I wanted to tail him but then I saw all the memorial decals along the back windshield dedicated to some relative. I thought, maybe I shouldn't; maybe he's in mourning. And then I thought, well, he had time to get those decals made, how fresh could it be? And then I thought, when isn't he in mourning though? And then I thought, when aren't we *all* in mourning? So I applied pressure to the gas pedal."

Her accomplice is stalling. The officers are blinking at him.

"Look, we have plenty more tangents where that came from," she adds.

Rampant notions are their specialty.

"And while I'm on the subject—" he attempts to cut back in.

"—It was simple. We broke in," she says. "At the rate we were going, we'd cover our debts in, I don't know, two or three lifetimes."

He was supposed to preside over the porch when they arrived but he became less of a guard and more of a Walmart greeter when neighbors started walking their dogs up and down the street.

Meanwhile, she was concocting a path to imagined treasure troves deposited throughout the house. But on her way through, the old lady announced herself.

"I've been expecting you," Mrs. Anderson said.

"What do you mean? How did you know?" she asked.

"That's what the others asked me too," Mrs. Anderson said.

She didn't want to assume but Mrs. Anderson didn't elaborate so she did anyway. It's probably because Mrs. Anderson owns this town. Like, she actually bought it. If she were Mrs. Anderson, she'd reasonably surmise that you don't leave a property like this and expect it to be there when you get back. In fact, Mrs. Anderson hadn't even left and here they were establishing themselves where they didn't belong.

"This place is basically a museum now," Mrs. Anderson sighed. "Still, these Milano cookies were half price this morning, and that's something. Can you believe it?"

She feigned a customary facial expression in response.

Back at the station, her accomplice says, "After we had given up, right when we thought she'd feed us to her swans, she offered us the pact."

"Mrs. Anderson looks right at him and admits that she is his secret admirer," she says.

He's been receiving unspeakable letters, crafts, shrines,

artfully positioned roadkill—the works—on his front stoop for years.

"But Mrs. Anderson doesn't stop there," she says. "Then, she tells us that 'according to vague calculations' she is a fortune teller, but only while she sleeps. I asked her if she ever tried to detect these abilities when fully awake and she said it was against her principles."

"Are you getting this down?" he asks one of the officers, who shifts in his seat.

"So I bet you're wondering about the pact. What it was and how it transpired. Basically, she agreed to tell our fortunes if we obliged her by tucking her in bed with some tea and a record full of plucked harp strings. And of course not pilfering any of her valuables. To seal the deal, she embroiders the scene of our pact, albeit a rather primitive rendering of the three of us hovering around her coffee table. Mrs. Anderson's pretty quick with a needle and thread," she continues.

That had really put a cap on the day. Mrs. Anderson had neglected to tell them that she snores her way through fortune telling, making crucial testaments challenging to decipher. They were able to get the gist.

Mrs. Anderson told the woman that one day she'd be sitting on a bench that was dedicated to herself, with a little plaque and everything. She told the man that he would die soon, but that "a funeral is the highest form of marketing."

Now he says to the cops, "None of that matters to me."

"And I guess somewhere along the way, nobody'd stopped her from picking up the phone and calling you guys, though I don't really see how we missed that," she says to the tirelessly tired officers in front of her.

At least the very last thing Mrs. Anderson ever told her, she keeps to herself. She said to the woman, "How much of knowing your future changes what you're doing?" And then, "Oh, your escorts have arrived."

LEAVE WELL ENOUGH
TOGETHER

———————————

There is a person running a marathon who collapses in the street. And there is a person who's the target of a professional hitman. And what you need to know is that this is the same person.

Long before an ambulance arranges itself beside the runner, a news van encircles the perimeter.

A couple decodes these events from a first-floor window. This window is cracked open. Their view is both better than the rest of the building's and worse, depending on what you're trying to witness.

"Here are these running enthusiasts you're always hearing about," the woman says.

She's momentarily uncooperative because she left her diary at a museum and someone returned it to her with commentary. Lo these many seconds ago, she buried it for safekeeping. She liquifies the root vegetables she calls her lunch while flailing her limbs in disapproval. Retribution would require unseemly amounts of effort since the most efficient route to the commenter involves flying hundreds of miles in the opposite direction.

Outside, a man looms above the runner. He claims to be psychic, waving around a special permit.

"It's a good thing this happened, you know," he says.

He leaves, only to return three minutes later offering hypnosis.

When an EMT steps forward, the man says, "Measures have already been taken."

A volunteer offers another runner a Dixie cup of chilled tap water.

"No thanks, I'm waiting for something better to come along."

Yet another participant appears to be rehearsing an anticipated conversation.

"Why would you think I'd do that? I'm not a controlled substance, so why would I expect them to work on me?"

This person then collects himself, observes the scene, and simulates reactions from the crowd.

The hitman hadn't planned on absconding from his trajectory, but even before the collapse, a cost-benefit analysis had proven his mission dubious. He is regarded in certain circles as untraceable. He has accumulated numerous ties to the community.

He approaches his intended victim as they bring out a stretcher.

"Listen, this isn't working out. It's never been a good fit. We both know you're perfectly capable of dying; it's not about that. You'll receive further instructions from me in three to five business days."

The runner nods. This runner is very understanding.

The hitman enters the nearest building.

"Do you validate?" he asks a woman in the lobby.

She confirms, escorting him to a desk.

He knocks on the couple's door afterward.

"Long time no see! What are you doing here?"

He steps inside and pulls a warm Power Bar sample from his pocket.

"Thanks. I'll put them with the others."

The couple has installed an aggressive amount of plaques on the walls. One reads: YOU HAVE ENTERED THE LIVING ROOM

"Care to join us in our weekly plaque-dusting venture?"

The hitman smiles, demurring.

Their conversation disintegrates.

He patrols the window. Bystanders begin spray-painting surrounding structures.

"What is with some people? I have little patience for vandalism."

They hand him drinks, snacks. They tamper with his thoughts.

"Did you come by for the race?" one tries.

"Why don't we leave well enough alo—together?" he says.

They are in the vicinity of snooping.

He redirects them with: "How did your art exhibition go?"

"We haven't spoken in years. And you remembered."

"I have a good memory for personal projects."

They huddle on a loveseat and await the evening news report.

Across town, our self-proclaimed soothsayer shouts "lonely" in a crowded theater, setting fire to his pride.

Grateful acknowledgment is made to the publications in which these works first appeared.

Chamber No. 1 was originally published in *New World Writing* as "Float."

Chamber No. 2 was originally published in *HAD* as "Echo Chamber."

Chamber No. 7 was originally published in *X-R-A-Y* as "The Dockmaster Must Never See This."

Chamber No. 8 was originally published in *The Rupture* as "Look at Her Now."

"Keel" was originally published in *Peach Mag*.

"Dredge" was originally published in *HAD*.

"You Can Renew Your Vows at Chuck E. Cheese Anytime You Like" was originally published in *Expat Lit Journal*.

"Empty Gestures" was originally published in *HAD*.

"Let the Groundhog Do the Talking" was originally published in *Wigleaf*.

"Best Available Human" was originally published in *Forever Mag*.

"Let's See That Again" was originally published in *No Contact*.

"Leave Well Enough Together" was originally published in *Ghost Parachute*.

"Feed Us to the Swans" was originally published in *Outlook Springs*.

Claire Hopple is the author of five books. Her fiction has appeared in *Wigleaf*, *Vol. 1 Brooklyn*, *Peach Mag*, *Forever Mag*, *HAD*, and others. She lives in Asheville, North Carolina. More at clairehopple.com.

OTHER VERY FINE TITLES FROM
TRIDENT PRESS

Blood-Soaked Buddha/Hard Earth Pascal
by Noah Cicero

it gets cold
by hazel avery

Major Diamonds Nights & Knives
by Katie Foster

Cactus
by Nathaniel Kennon Perkins

The Pocket Emma Goldman

Sixty Tattoos I Secretly Gave Myself at Work
by Tanner Ballengee

The Pocket Peter Kropotkin

The Silence is the Noise
by Bart Schaneman

The Pocket Aleister Crowley

Propaganda of the Deed:
The Pocket Alexander Berkman

Los Espiritus
by Josh Hyde

The Soul of Man Under Socialism
by Oscar Wilde

The Pocket Austin Osman Spare

www.tridentcafe.com/trident-press-titles